AKIMBA
AND THE
MAGIC COW

AKIMBA AND THE MAGIC COW

A FOLKTALE FROM AFRICA

Retold by ANNE ROSE

Woodcuts by HOPE MERYMAN

SCHOLASTIC BOOK SERVICES

NEW YORK • TORONTO • LONDON • AUCKLAND • SYDNEY • TOKYO

Text copyright © 1976 by Anne Rose. Illustrations copyright © 1976 by Hope Meryman. All rights reserved. Published by Scholastic Book Services, a division of Scholastic Magazines, Inc.

12 11 10 9 8 7 6 5 4 3 2   9/7 0 1/8

Printed in the U.S.A.

to Sonja and Alexander

Anne Rose

to Bernice, Mary Jane and Dick

Hope Meryman

Akimba was the poorest man in his village.
One morning he had nothing left to eat —
not even a crumb.
"I have no food and I have no money.
I must leave the village," Akimba thought,
"and see what I can do."

So Akimba set out.

Soon he came to a deep forest.

He saw an old man chopping firewood.

Akimba helped him stack the logs.

"Where are you going?" the old man asked.

"I have no food and I have no money.

I must see what I can do," Akimba said.

"Maybe I can help you," said the old man.

"Behind this bush you'll find a cow.
Take her home with you and say 'kukuku.'
Say 'kukuku' to her and see what happens."

So Akimba took the cow and went back to his hut.

"Kukuku," he said to her.

The cow opened her mouth and a gold coin
fell out.

"Wah!" cried Akimba. "Kukuku! Kukuku!"

And in no time at all, Akimba was rich.

One day Akimba had to go on a long journey.
He could not take his cow with him.
So he went to see his good neighbor Bumba.
"Bumba," he said, "will you keep my cow
for me? She's no trouble as long as you
don't say 'kukuku' to her.
'Kukuku' is the one thing you must never say."

"Very well," Bumba said. "I will do as you wish."
So Akimba gave Bumba the cow and went down the road.

The very moment Akimba was gone,
Bumba ran up to the cow.
"Kukuku," he said.
To his amazement the cow opened her mouth
and a gold coin fell out.
"Kukuku," Bumba said again.
Another coin fell to the ground.
"Wah!" cried Bumba. "This cow is good
to have and better yet to keep."

A few days later, Akimba came back.
"Where is my cow?" he asked.

"Here she is," Bumba said.
But he gave Akimba another cow instead.

Akimba took the cow home and said, "Kukuku."
"Moo-oo," said the cow. But nothing happened.

"Have you forgotten your master's voice?"
Akimba shouted. "Kuku, kukuku!"

"Moo-oo, moooo-oooo," mooed the cow.
But no gold coins came.

So Akimba went to find the old man in the woods.

"My cow stopped giving gold," Akimba said.
"Soon I will be hungry again."

"Behind this bush you'll find a sheep.
Take her home with you and say 'bururu.'
Say 'bururu' to her and see what happens."

So Akimba took the sheep
and went back to his hut.

"Bururu," he said to her.

The sheep opened her mouth and a silver
coin fell out.
"Wah!" Akimba shouted. "Bururu, bururu!"
And in no time at all, Akimba was rich.

But the day came when Akimba had to leave
on another journey.
He brought his sheep to his good neighbor Bumba.
"Bumba," he asked, "will you keep my sheep
for me? She's no trouble as long as you
don't say 'bururu' to her.
'Bururu' is the one thing you must never say."

"Very well," Bumba said. "I will do as you wish."

The moment Akimba was gone, Bumba ran
to the sheep.
"Bururu!" he said.
The sheep opened her mouth. A silver coin
fell out.

"Wah!" Bumba shouted. "This sheep is
good to have and better yet to keep."

A few weeks later, Akimba came back.
"Where is my sheep?" he asked.

"Here she is," said Bumba.
But he gave Akimba another sheep instead.

Akimba hurried home.
"Bururu," he said to the sheep.

"Baa, baa," said the sheep.
But no silver coins fell.

"Bururu! Bururu!" Akimba shouted.
Still no silver coins!

"This sheep has turned deaf in my absence,"
said Akimba.

And he went to find the old man in the woods.

"My sheep stopped giving silver," Akimba said.
"Soon I'll be hungry as before."

"There is a chicken behind this bush.
Take her with you," said the old man.
"When you get home, say 'klaklakla' to her,
Say 'klaklakla' and see what happens."

So Akimba got the chicken and took her home.

"Klaklakla," he said to her.

The chicken laid an egg.

"What?" yelled Akimba. "No silver? No gold?"

"Klaklakla," he shouted.

The chicken laid more eggs.

"Well," said Akimba, "eggs are eggs."

And he ate them.

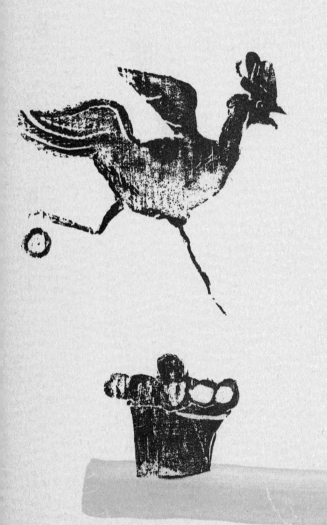

The next time Akimba was called away,
he asked Bumba to keep his chicken.

"She's no trouble as long as you don't
say 'klaklakla' to her. 'Klaklakla' is
the one thing you must never say."

"Do not worry," Bumba said.
"I will be more than glad to keep your chicken."

As soon as Akimba was out of sight, Bumba
ran to the chicken.

"Klaklakla!" he shouted.
The chicken laid an egg.

"Fooh!" cried Bumba.
"No gold? No silver? Only eggs?"
"Oh well," he thought, "eggs are eggs."
And he ate them.

And when Akimba came back and asked for his
chicken, Bumba gave him another one instead.

So Akimba went to see the old man in the
woods again.

"My cow stopped giving gold," he cried.
"My sheep stopped giving silver.
Even my chicken stopped laying eggs.
Soon I will be hungry as before."

"There's a stick behind this bush," the
old man said. "Go home and tell it to
dance for you. When you want it to stop,
shout 'mulu.'"

"Thank you," said Akimba, and he took the stick.

As soon as he was home, he told the stick
to dance. But the stick did not dance.
It jumped up and beat him instead.

Akimba was so surprised he almost forgot
the magic word.
"Mulu!" he yelled at last, and the stick
fell to the floor.

Akimba looked at the stick for a long time.
"Humm," he thought. "I must pay another
visit to Bumba."

Then Akimba took the stick to Bumba's house.

"Bumba," he said, "I have to leave again.
Will you keep my stick for me?"

"Well, well," Bumba thought.
"The cow brought me gold.
The sheep brought me silver.
The chicken brought me eggs.
Who knows what the stick will bring?"

And he grabbed the stick and pushed Akimba
out the door.

Akimba turned around.
"I almost forgot," he said.
"Do not say 'Stick, dance for me.'
Remember, whatever you do, do not ask
the stick to dance."

The moment Akimba was out of sight, Bumba yelled,
"Stick, dance for me!"

And the stick jumped up. But it did not dance.
It beat him and beat him and would not stop.

The stick was still hitting Bumba
when Akimba came back.

"Now will you give me my true cow and
my true sheep and my true chicken?" Akimba asked.

"Anything!" cried Bumba.
"Just stop this stick from beating me!"

"Mulu," Akimba said.
And the stick fell to the floor.

Akimba picked up the stick.
He took his true cow and his true sheep.
He took his true chicken.
Then he went back to his hut.

"Klaklakla," he said to his chicken.
Akimba's plate was filled with eggs.

"Bururu," he said to his sheep.
And silver coins clanked to the floor.

"Kukuku," he said to his cow.
And gold coins piled up to the roof.

Akimba never had to go hungry again.